rh

Fuzz McFlops

EVA FURNARI

Translated from the Portuguese
by Alison Entrekin

Pushkin Children's Books

Pushkin Children's Books
71–75 Shelton Street,
London WC2H 9JQ

Text and Illustrations © Eva Furnari 2006

Rights to this edition negotiated via Seibel Publishing Services

English translation © Alison Entrekin 2015

Fuzz McFlops first published in Portuguese as
Felpo Filva by Moderna in 2006

This translation first published by Pushkin Children's Books in 2015

Work published with the support of the Brazilian
Ministry of Culture / National Library Foundation

Obra publicada com o apoio do Ministério da Cultura
do Brasil / Fundação Biblioteca Nacional

MINISTÉRIO DA CULTURA
Fundação BIBLIOTECA NACIONAL

0 0 1

ISBN 978 1 782690 75 7

Printed in China by WKT Co

www.pushkinchildrens.com

THIS STORY IS DEDICATED
TO EVERYONE
WITH DIFFERENT EARS.

In Burrow 88, Briar Road, Swifton, lived a very reclusive rabbit. He didn't receive any visitors, had no friends, and was never interested in talking to anyone.

His neighbours were used to it and said he was scatterbrained and spacey, with his head in the clouds, but it was understandable, because he was a poet.

He was the famous poet and writer Fuzz McFlops.

Fuzz had been a loner ever since he was a little rabbit, when his classmates used to tease him for having one ear shorter than the other.

Being different had always been a problem, and things got even worse when it was decided that Fuzz would have to wear a special device to stretch out his short ear.

It was called an Earlongator. It was large, heavy and awkward. And, worst of all, it made no difference. All his suffering was in vain. No one knew exactly why, but the device, which worked so well on other young bunnies, didn't on Fuzz. His short ear stayed short.

One day, when Fuzz was already a famous poet, he decided to tell everyone his sad life story. He was going to write his autobiography.

The rabbit writer made himself a cup of coffee, sat down in front of his typewriter and began:

```
Chapter 1 - Childhood

    My name is Fuzz. I am a poet and a writer.
I am a loner and don't like to leave my burrow.
When I was young, I had a hard time because
one of my ears was shorter than the other.
My classmates always made fun of me...
```

Fuzz remembered an old piece of paper that had been in his drawer for the longest time, and placed it on the desk next to the typewriter. It was the instruction manual for the Earlongator. It reminded him of his childhood.

Bunny Perfection Earlongator

Instruction Manual

INTRODUCTION

The BUNNY PERFECTION EARLONGATOR is designed for young rabbits who suffer from asymmetrical auricular dysmorphology. The objective of the device is to stretch the shorter ear while the rabbit is growing. It should be used for at least 5 years.

Masterscrew to hold ear in place

Metal frame with side adjustment

Crank for stretch control

Helmet fastener

USE

Users should not remove the device to sleep or bathe. After bathing, the ears should be thoroughly dried with _Bunny Perfection Cotton Swabs*_ to avoid watearitis.

WARNING

It is recommended that users do not play football, chase or hide-and-seek, as they may hurt their friends with the device.

*_Bunny Perfection Cotton Swabs_, now with _supersuckyuppy_, _ultrafluff_ cotton tips, are available in hard and flexible models, in a range of colours, thicknesses and lengths.

TECHNICAL SUPPORT

For operational queries or faulty equipment, please call our Cottontail Service Department's 24-hour hareline.

At that moment, his thoughts were interrupted by the doorbell. It was the post-bunny, with an enormous pile of letters. Fuzz received lots, but he never read them. In fact, he didn't even open them and just tossed them in a trunk.

This day, however, one envelope caught Fuzz's eye: it was large, violet and tied with a silk ribbon. He opened it and read:

Fuzz McFlops
Burrow 88, Briar Road,
Swifton

20TH February

Dear Mr McFlops,
My name is Charlotte and I am a great admirer of your
talent and poems, but, if you will allow me, there are
a few that I don't like at all. I really have a problem
with the story of the 'Back-to-Front Princess'! For
heaven's sake, what a dreadful ending! Here it is:

The back-to-front princess
lives not in a tower.
The bottom of the well's
her uncomfortable lair.

She waits for prince charming,
who isn't all that bright,
to toss her a rope,
rather than let down her hair.

When the moment arrives,
the back-to-front maiden,
with a tug and a topple,
her prince doth ensnare.

Cold, and rather hungry,
the unfortunate couple
live unhappily
ever after, down there.

WITH ALL DUE RESPECT, IT'S SUCH A PESSIMISTIC STORY!
I HATE THE SAD, DRAMATIC ENDING. THE POOR THINGS!
PLEASE FIND BELOW MY CONTINUATION OF THE POEM,
IN WHICH I HAVE CHANGED THEIR FATE.

> NO ONE KNOWS HOW IT HAPPENED,
> BUT SALVATION WAS NIGH.
> OUT OF THE BLUE THERE CAME
> AN ANSWER TO THEIR PRAYERS.

> THEY BID THE WELL GOODBYE,
> WITH ITS SMELL OF MOULD
> AND ITS LAYER OF SCUM:
> A TRULY GLOOMY AFFAIR.

> THEY PACKED UP THEIR JUNK,
> BELONGINGS AND KIDS,
> AND IN A JET PLANE
> THEY TOOK TO THE AIR.

> THEY WENT NOT TO A TOWER,
> AND NOT TO THE MOON.
> ON THE EARTH THEY STAYED,
> FEET PLANTED, FAIR AND SQUARE.

> THEY BOUGHT A LOVELY HOUSE
> OVERLOOKING THE SEA
> AND LIVED FOREVER
> BY THE BEACH, IN DECK CHAIRS.

WHAT DO YOU THINK? THEY'LL BE MUCH
HAPPIER NOW, WON'T THEY?
I HOPE YOU'RE NOT OFFENDED BY THIS.

> YOURS FAITHFULLY,
> CHARLOTTE PASSE-PARTOUT

When Fuzz finished reading, his right ear (the short one) started to twitch. Whenever he got upset his ear would twitch uncontrollably. Unfortunately, besides having one ear shorter than the other, he also suffered from earspasmitis.

The letter had really distressed Fuzz. A famous rabbit like him wasn't used to people saying they didn't like his work so blatantly.

Who was that Charlotte, who had the courage to talk to him like that? And to change the end of his story to boot? What cheek! Fuzz decided not to dignify her letter with a reply. He screwed it up and threw it away.

The letter ended up in the bin, but not its contents. Fuzz couldn't forget what Charlotte had said. Was it possible that she was right? Was he really that pessimistic?

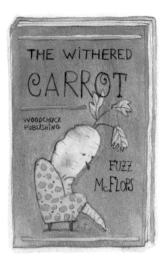

He thought about the titles of his books: *The Withered Carrot, The Veggie Patch Behind Bars, Red Eyes, The Unlucky Rabbit's Foot, Unhappy Easter.*

He began to question himself. He fished the letter out of the bin, smoothed it out, and read and reread it about fifteen times. Now that he thought about it, Charlotte's sincerity was actually a good thing. It's easier to trust people who speak their mind. He put the creased letter in his desk drawer.

It took Fuzz a good while to forget the matter but when he finally did, another violet envelope arrived. He read the letter.

3ᴿᴰ MAY

DEAR POET,

BECAUSE YOU DIDN'T ANSWER ME, I AM WRITING AGAIN.
YOU KNOW THAT POEM OF YOURS, 'BIRDS IN CAGES'? IF I'M
TO BE REALLY HONEST, I THINK IT'S LACKING SOMEWHAT IN
FREEDOM, JOY AND IMAGINATION! I'LL TRY TO EXPLAIN.
YOUR POEM GOES LIKE THIS:

> PILLOWS HAVE FEATHERS
> BIRDS DO TOO.

> PILLOWS HAVE BEDS
> BIRDS, NOT TRUE.

> PITCHERS HAVE BEAKS
> BIRDS DO TOO.

> PITCHERS HAVE FRESH WATER
> BIRDS, NOT TRUE.

> PLANES HAVE WINGS
> BIRDS DO TOO.

> PLANES HAVE THE SKIES
> BIRDS, NOT TRUE.

I TOOK THE LIBERTY TO REWRITE YOUR POEM, SETTING THE BIRDS FREE. AND IT TURNED OUT LIKE THIS:

BIRDS WITHOUT CAGES

DOGS HAVE BONES
BIRDS DO TOO.

WINDOWS HAVE BARS
BIRDS, NOT TRUE.

CHAIRS HAVE LEGS
BIRDS DO TOO.

HARES HAVE TEETH
BIRDS, NOT TRUE.

FRYING PANS HAVE EGGS
BIRDS DO TOO.

BURROWS HAVE OWNERS
BIRDS, NOT TRUE.

DON'T YOU THINK IT'S MORE INTERESTING LIKE THIS?
DON'T YOU AGREE THAT THE BIRDS ARE FREER AND HAPPIER?

YOURS SINCERELY,
    CHARLOTTE

P.S. — HE WHO PLANTS EGGS REAPS BIRDS.

He who plants eggs reaps birds? That Charlotte was crazy! She'd had the audacity to rewrite his poem and to suggest that he had no imagination!!! This time she had gone too far! Fuzz wasn't amused. He was indignant, very indignant, and wrote back immediately:

```
Charlotte,

     You are entirely
mistaken about me.
I have a lot of
imagination - you have
no idea how much. This
is how I imagine you:
bloated belly, hairy
ears, bulbous nose,
droopy whiskers.


     Yours,
     Fuzz McFlops, a very imaginative poet.
```

As soon as he had finished writing the letter, Fuzz went out and posted it. He returned home feeling smug. He had given that cheeky rabbit the answer she deserved!

Half an hour later, however, his right ear began to twitch. He was beginning to second-guess himself. Should he have answered her like that? He reread her version of the bird poem. It wasn't that bad... He had to admit that Charlotte had a certain flair for writing and quite a sense of humour.

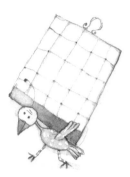

He wondered if she wrote her own poems. And also what she would think of his latest book, *The Sad Warren*.

Fuzz thought about these things for days, but he didn't have any answers. Until a telegram arrived, a week later.

```
12/05

SWIFTON


POET IF YOU THINK I LOOK LIKE THAT THEN

COME SEE FOR YOURSELF STOP COME HAVE A CUP

OF TEA AND CARROT CAKE WITH ME IN MY BURROW

STOP YOU CAN PICK THE DAY STOP THERE IS

NONE SO BLIND AS HE WHO REFUSES TO SEE HIS

OWN IMAGINATION STOP CHARLOTTE
```

As he stared at the brazen invitation, Fuzz's right ear began to twitch. He was really worked up. He didn't know what was worse: leaving his burrow, telling her he liked her poems, having tea with someone he didn't know or eating carrot cake, which he hated.

Fuzz didn't know what to do. He was so confused that he had an attack of acute earspasmitis.

He got his medicine box, where he kept all kinds of things to treat earspasmitis. He looked for a bottle of Twitchannul, medication for out-of-control ears. He was terrified of side effects, so he read the patient information leaflet three times, then took two spoonfuls and went to bed.

TWITCHANNUL™

INTRODUCTION
Oral suspension - bottle contains 200 ml
FOR ADULTS
SHAKE BEFORE USE

COMPOSITION
1 tablespoon contains:

vehicle q.s	.14.5 ml
desmyelotine	0.3 ml
quivrelax	0.1 ml
mipropyleneglyeol	0.1 ml

DISCLAIMER
Twitchannul™ is to be taken orally in the case of nervous earspasmitis. It is not a cure; it only controls twitching. Patients should seek other forms of treatment to cure themselves of the condition.

INDICATION
For the temporary relief of symptoms of mild and monstrous earspasmitis.

WARNING
If, after ingestion, the patient turns green or experiences an unbearably itchy nose, he or she is allergic to the medication and should suspend use immediately.

CAUTION
Twitchannul™ should not be taken in cases of contagious earachy runnynosis, as it can mask the symptoms.
It should not be taken during pregnancy.

DOSAGE
For mild earspasmitis, take one tablespoon.
For monstrous earspasmitis, take two tablespoons.

OVERDOSE
In the event of an overdose, it is recommended that the patient stop being a twit and never do it again.

KEEP OUT OF REACH OF BABY BUNNIES.

INTOX LABORATORIES
Head pharmacist: Alpha Carotene - Reg. #49866

See box for batch number, fabrication and expiry dates.

The next day, Fuzz was already much calmer and his earspasmitis was almost under control. When he mustered up the courage, he got a piece of paper and wrote:

Charlotte,

I really like your sincerity. I would like
to be sincere with you too. Therefore, I must
say up front that I have a lot of flaws (big
ones and huge ones). To explain them, here
is a fable:

THE HARE AND THE TORTOISE
One day, the hare said to the tortoise:
'I feel sorry for you, having to carry your
house around on your back. You can't run, play
or flee from your enemies.'
The tortoise thought for a moment, then replied:
'Hare, it is true that I am slow and heavy.
And I won't deny that you are light and fast.
But save your pity. Let's have a race and see
who crosses the finish line first, you or me.'
The hare thought it was hilarious and
accepted the challenge right then and there.
They decided where the race would start and end.
As soon as it began, the tortoise set off.
Seeing how slow and heavy he was, the hare
began to laugh, leap about and make fun of him.
Meanwhile, the tortoise kept moving forward at
his sleepy pace.
'Hey, pal!' laughed the hare, 'Don't run so
much! You'll wear yourself out! I think I'll
have a rest.' And to tease him even more, he
pretended to fall asleep and snore. He pretended

so hard that he fell asleep for real, and when he
opened his eyes he saw the tortoise far off in
the distance, almost at the finish line. The hare
dashed after him as fast as he could go, but it
was too late. The tortoise won the race. And the
hare, who was so quick, lost.

MORAL OF THE STORY:
Slow and steady wins
the race, especially if
your opponent takes a nap.

So, Charlotte, I'm slow, very slow. I do
everything slowly. I confess: I'm a rabbit with
the soul of a tortoise.

Like tortoises, I don't like going out much.
I only go to the post office and the market.
I hate carrots. My favourite food is chocolate
balls and only if they're like the ones my
grandma used to make. And there's more: I suffer
from earspasmitis and one of my ears is shorter
than the other.

As you can see, I'd best not accept your
invitation. And if I eventually do, the decision
may take years.

Farewell,
Fuzz

There. It hadn't been easy, but Fuzz had managed to write the letter and had been sincere. He'd poured his heart out, even though he was pretty sure Charlotte wouldn't want anything more to do with him after that.

And now that the matter was resolved, he could go back to writing his book.

Fuzz tried. Once, twice, many times, but he couldn't. He wasn't able to focus on the task at hand. All he could think about was Charlotte and what she would think of him after reading his letter.

Instead of working on his book, Fuzz spent days writing other things: poems, texts, phrases. And, in the midst of it all, he surprised himself by writing something very different to what he usually wrote: a fairytale.

A RATHER WEIRD STORY

Once upon a time there was a prince who was different to other princes. He was rather ugly, rather strange, rather lopsided and rather unlucky too.

One day, the prince was locked in a tower by a horrible princess, who was bossy, boring and frightful-looking to boot. The poor prince felt awful, worse than a toad in the desert.

Luckily, a very interesting witch, who was pretty, cheerful and had a great sense of humour, heard of the prince's plight. She lost no time, mounted her horse on her back and raced to the tower.

When she got there, she cried:

'Oh, beloved prince, let down your hair! I have come to save you!'

The prince was so happy at her arrival that, without thinking, he leapt from the tower. He fell on the horse, broke a leg, his two front teeth, twisted his ribs, tore his clothes and, as if all that weren't enough, he lost his wig too. Nobody knows what became of the poor horse.

The prince was a right mess, but the witch, who loved him, took such good care of him that he got better, though he was a little more lopsided than before.

The witch and the prince moved to a faraway land, which was much more beautiful than the one they were in, and bought a gorgeous old castle on a mountaintop. And then, the thing that no one believed could happen actually happened: they lived happily ever after, with lots of love.

THE END

FOOTNOTE: One day, when they were very old and still happy, they heard that the wicked princess had married a dragon. A fire-breathing dragon who had sent her evil up in smoke.

Fuzz was pleased with the result and had a great time writing it, which was most unusual. He had proven that he was capable of writing funny, optimistic things. He wanted to send the story to Charlotte. While he was mustering up the courage to do so, another letter arrived from her.

23ʳᵈ MAY

DEAR FUZZ,

I WAS MOVED BY YOUR LETTER.

I LIKE DIFFERENT EARS. I THINK THEY LEND A CERTAIN CHARM TO A RABBIT. YOU OF ALL RABBITS, BEING A POET, SHOULD PRIDE YOURSELF ON BEING SPECIAL.

IT WAS BEAUTIFUL AND COURAGEOUS OF YOU TO CONFESS THAT YOU HAVE THE SOUL OF A TORTOISE. AFTER ALL, THEY ARE VERY WISE.

IMAGINE IF YOU WERE A RABBIT WITH THE SOUL OF A BUZZARD? REMEMBER THAT SAYING: POOR OLD BUZZARD, WITH A FATE SO BLEAK, WHEN HE FALLS OFF HIS PERCH, HE BREAKS HIS BEAK? THAT WOULD BE UNFORTUNATE...

WELL, FUZZ, NOW I ADMIRE NOT ONLY YOUR POEMS, BUT YOU AS A RABBIT TOO. IF AND WHEN YOU WANT TO COME HAVE A CUP OF TEA WITH ME, YOU ARE MORE THAN WELCOME.

I LOVE TO COOK AND AM CURIOUS TO TRY YOUR GRANDMA'S CHOCOLATE BALLS. COULD YOU SEND ME THE RECIPE?

YOURS,
CHARLOTTE

Fuzz read the letter. He felt his left ear twitch. That hadn't happened in a long time. The right one twitched whenever he was upset (he was used to that), but the left one only twitched when he was happy, and that was much rarer.

He looked for a mirror. He rummaged through the whole house until he found an old one, forgotten at the bottom of a drawer. He put on his best poet's face and looked at himself.

Then he got his notebook of recipes from the kitchen. He sat at his desk and wrote:

Charlotte,
Here is my grandma's recipe.

CHOCOLATE BALLS
Ingredients:
1/2 tin of condensed milk
150g of crumbled coconut biscuits
100g of powdered chocolate

Instructions:
     Stir the chocolate into the condensed milk,
then add the crumbled biscuits and mix well.
Leave in fridge for 15 minutes to harden. Roll
into medium-size balls. After that, enjoy.

I hope you like it as much as I do.
Do you write poems too?
Yours,
Fuzz

Fuzz raced to the post office to send the letter and returned home feeling light-hearted. Half an hour later, however, he was flustered again. He had forgotten to say a whole bunch of things in his letter.

During the week, he made a list of all the things he didn't want to forget in his next letter:

1. Thank her again for her invitation and explain that it will take me more than a year to MAYBE accept it.

2. Send her 'A RATHER WEIRD STORY'.

3. Ask her to send a picture of herself.

4. Ask if she collects proverbs.

5. Ask if she has a boyfriend.

Every day, he checked the mail for a violet envelope. Finally, on a very rainy day, a postcard arrived, sopping wet.

DEAR FUZZ

SOON COME

SWALLOWED

PIANO

HELP

CHARLOTTE

FUZZ McFLOPS
BURROW 88
BRIAR ROAD
SWIFTON

When he read those terrible words, Fuzz didn't think twice. He checked Charlotte's address and raced out the door, without a raincoat or umbrella. Luckily, she didn't live very far away.

He ran as fast as he could, imagining her choking on the piano, barely able to breathe, in urgent need of his help. But he, Fuzz Loopy La-La McFlops, the poet, was there to save her from a tragic end!

Like a hurricane, he blew in without knocking and almost bowled down the door. He tripped over a chair and landed with a thud at the foot of the sofa where she was sitting. Panting and dishevelled, clothes splattered with mud, he peered up at her from the floor.

'Charlotte?'

'Fuzz?'

Charlotte had green cream on her shins and a grey paste on her eyebrows and ears. She was dying her fur and waxing her legs. The old t-shirt she was wearing had holes in it and it was smudged with dye.

She leapt behind the sofa to hide. Fuzz would think she was ugly, sloppy and poorly dressed and would know she dyed her fur and waxed her legs. From behind the sofa she cried:

'Fuzz, you came without letting me know?'

'Um... I got your postcard asking for help... Didn't you swallow a piano? I came... to save you... ...Look, it's written here...'

Fuzz held out the wet postcard and she took it. After a moment of silence, Charlotte burst out laughing so hard that she couldn't contain herself. Forgetting her creams, she came out from behind the sofa.

The colour drained from Fuzz's face. Something wasn't right. She hadn't swallowed a piano! And he had burst into her house like a mad-rabbit. She must think he was crazy. His right ear began to twitch wildly. He got ready to run away, but Charlotte didn't let him. She grabbed him by the arm, took her mouth guard out in front of him and explained, with tears in her eyes from laughing so hard, that the rain had smudged most of the message and it had turned out completely different to the original, which said:

'I hope you **come** have tea with me **soon**.
I tried your grandma's recipe and loved it!
I practically **swallowed** the chocolate balls
in one sitting.

I write poems, but only occasionally.
I play the **piano** and compose songs.
If you do come have tea with me one day,
I hope you can **help** me write some
lyrics for my melodies.'

When Fuzz McFlops heard that, he cracked up laughing too. They both hooted with laughter and didn't stop for a long while.

They didn't have tea or chocolate balls that day, but they did the next. Fuzz was smartly dressed and smelling nice and Charlotte was dressed up to the nines.

The poet left his burrow many times to visit Charlotte.

After many many cups of tea, chocolate balls and poems, he started to feel at home at her place.

One day, they wrote a song together.

On another occasion, Fuzz gave Charlotte a short story he had written just for her: 'Two Rabbits in a Hat'.

When Charlotte finished reading it she had tears in her eyes. She gave Fuzz a kiss and asked for his paw in marriage. He fainted and was so happy that he had an attack of earspasmitis atrox in his left ear.

When he recovered, he married Charlotte, with lots of love.

THE END

P.S.*

'Is that the end of the story?'

'Yep. There are just a
few comments in the
next few pages.'

'Gossip about the characters?'

'I wish... but no. They're
comments about the kinds
of text used in the story.'

'What for?'

'I dunno. It wasn't my idea.'

'So what are we doing
here, then?'

'Dunno. I was sent here
to say this, so I came.'

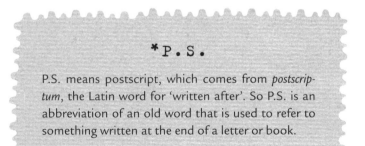

*P.S.

P.S. means postscript, which comes from *postscriptum*, the Latin word for 'written after'. So P.S. is an abbreviation of an old word that is used to refer to something written at the end of a letter or book.

'Ah, so P.S. is something you write when you're done?'

'I guess so...'

'So, in fact, you're not really done!'

'I guess not...'

'Kind of like dessert.'

'Dessert?'

'Yeah, when you've eaten your dinner, you're done, but not really. It's time for...'

'...pudding and sweets!!!'

'P.S.!!!'

PRESENTERS

'When I grow up I'm going to write a borography — the story of a bore.'

'And I'm going to write a liography — a story full of lies.'

'And I'm going to invent a cakograph — a device for writing on cakes.'

CHARLOTTE'S NIECES →

AUTOBIOGRAPHY

When someone writes their own story, they are creating a text called an autobiography. Breaking the word into parts: *auto* means 'own', *bio* means 'life' and *graphy* means 'to write', so it is writing about one's own life.

'Tortoise, I'm worried about my image. After that fable, people have been saying bad things about me.'

'You should stop worrying about what others think and spend more time on self-development.'

'Self-development?'

'Why don't you come to the lecture I'm giving tomorrow? It's about the difference between slowness and laziness. Ah, and after the interval the sloth is going to give a sensational performance!'

'Hmm...'

THE HARE

AND THE TORTOISE

FABLE

A fable is a story that teaches a moral or behavioural lesson. There is often a sentence at the end called the 'moral of the story', that is, the lesson in a nutshell. The characters tend to be talking animals that relate to one another like human beings. Fables show that qualities such as kindness, honesty, prudence and hard work are better than selfishness, cruelty, envy and greed.

'Fairytales are basically Tales of Mother Goose.'

'Goose tails? I thought they were fairies' tails.'

'Fairies don't have tails.'

'Dog-fairies do.'

'Is there a such thing as a dog-fairy?'

'Of course! Just like bunny-fairies...'

'Hmm...'

ANOTHER NIECE AND NEPHEW

FAIRYTALE

A fairytale is generally a short story in which the hero or heroine faces great obstacles before triumphing over evil. The plot usually involves things like fantastical beings, magic, metamorphoses and spells. Common characters are princes, princesses, fairies, witches and dragons.

'I wonder if that saying "A restless or twitching eye or lip betrays the condition of the heart" applies to Fuzz's ears.'

'You're terrible. That's mean!'

'No, it isn't. That proverb that goes "A bird in the hand is worth two in the bush" is mean!'

'True. Feathered Rights activists should get it banned.'

'So they should!'

← LITTLE BIRDS

PROVERBS AND SAYINGS

Proverbs and sayings are usually short phrases, passed down by word of mouth, which sum up an idea, a social custom, or popular advice. In most cases, no one knows who made them up.

'I don't get why some little birds go to jail if they haven't committed a crime. Do you?'

'Nope.'

'Do you know why, in Charlotte's poem, the birds with bones are freer? I didn't get that bit.'

'Me neither.'

THE SAME LITTLE BIRDS

POEM

A poem is a text in verse that has its own musicality, created by the sounds of the words. The meter is provided by the number of syllables in each line, and rhymes are important to its overall sound. But not all poems are like this; some don't have any rhyme or meter. They are called free verse poems.

Writing poems is a way of playing with words, creating relationships between meaning, sound and form.

'I'm so sad "The Opposite of the Tower" was cut from the book. It's his best poem...'

'How does it go again?'

'I'll recite it:

"The tower is high,
deep is the well.

In the tower you cry,
in the well you do too.

The tower is dry,
wet is the well.

From the tower you fly,
from the well you do too.

Soar in the sky,
wish in the well.

Bid the tower bye-bye,
and the well you do too."'

'What a beauty!'

'It is indeed!'

'Who's Indeed? Is she that long-legged lass from Burrow 78?'

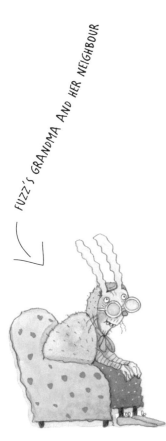

FUZZ'S GRANDMA AND HER NEIGHBOUR

46

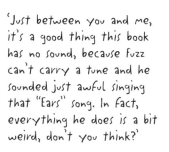

'Just between you and me, it's a good thing this book has no sound, because Fuzz can't carry a tune and he sounded just awful singing that "Ears" song. In fact, everything he does is a bit weird, don't you think?'

SONG

A song is a composition that combines a melody with a poem – the lyrics. The melody is notated in a score, which is a written record of the notes, tempo and intensity with which it should be played.

'There are serious problems with this story. I think the mail should be delivered by a messenger pigeon rather than a post-bunny.'

'But he looks so good in the illustration.'

'Well I don't think he should have such a big illustration! He isn't at all important to the story.'

'True...'

'And I think the rules of letter writing are silly.'

'How do you write a letter?'

'I start by saying goodbye and then write the rest in the P.S.'

A MESSENGER PIGEON AND AN OWL

LETTER

Sending a letter is an old-fashioned way to get a message to someone. Letters can be written in a variety of ways, but they tend to follow a traditional layout. Normally, you start with the address of the person to whom you are writing, and then the date. Then you write their name, followed by the letter itself, and finish with a word or phrase such as 'Yours faithfully', 'Yours sincerely', 'Yours' or 'Love' (depending on how well you know the person), and your signature.

Letters are delivered by the postal services of different countries, and they have created a few rules and conventions (such as post codes) to ensure your letter gets to its destination quickly. In the United States of America, the post code is called a ZIP code, which stands for 'Zone Improvement Plan'. Envelopes with ZIP codes on them are generally delivered faster – or more *zippily!*

TELEGRAM

A telegram is a message transmitted by telegraph, which reaches its recipient quickly. In the past, when someone wanted to send a super urgent message, they would send a telegram, because ordinary letters took a long time to reach their destination. A few countries still offer telegram services, but nowadays there are many other ways to send a message quickly, such as e-mail and text messages.

'Did you know what ZIP meant?'

'Nope. I always thought it was a code for zips!'

'And I thought it stood for Zery Important Person.'

TWIN NEPHEWS

POSTCARD

A postcard is a type of correspondence that is usually sent without an envelope. There is generally a picture on one side, while the other has space for a postage stamp, the receiver's address, and a short message from the sender.

'LLoooooooooolllllaaaaa, ccaaaaaaannnnn
yyyyoooooovvvvvvv vvvnpppplluvvvvvggg
tthhiiiiiiissss pppppplllleeeeaaaaassssssssssssee?'

'I told you to read the instruction manual
before using those thermal trousers, didn't I?
But you're so stubborn... you didn't listen.'

ANOTHER NIECE AND NEPHEW

INSTRUCTION MANUAL

An instruction manual is a booklet that explains
how to use a machine, an electronic device, a
household appliance, a game or a toy. To be
clear, manuals are usually divided into parts.
They often contain illustrations, as certain
things are easier to understand with the help of
a picture.

DR ALPHA CAROTENE

'I am shy and modest, but I know that some people would like to meet me, so I am here to introduce myself: Dr Alpha Carotene, the head pharmacist at Intox. I have just published my autobiography, A Life of Injections, which is on sale in the best pharmacies. In it, I explain how I became so successful, rich, handsome, young and happily married to Mrs Beta Carotene.'

PATIENT INFORMATION

Patient information is a sheet of instructions that comes with a medication and states its composition, method of use, warnings, manufacturer and other important information.

'I made Grandma Filva's recipe.'

'Did it turn out well?'

'It did, but we had a problem later.'

'What?'

'The balls got stuck in little Zenny's braces and he couldn't open his mouth for half an hour.'

RECIPE

A recipe explains how to make a certain kind of food. It starts with a list of ingredients and the amounts to be used. Amounts can be expressed as weight, volume, number of items, size – or even handfuls and pinches. The second part tells you how to prepare the food, step by step. At the end there is generally a comment on how to present it and how many people it serves.

'When I grow up, I want to be an Easter Bunny. I've heard that in order to be good one, you can't scramble your eggs. An Easter Bunny has a long list of requests and he has to get them just right.

THE POST-BUNNY'S SON

LIST

A list is a sequence of items. People write them for many different reasons: to remember names, to remind themselves of things to do or things to buy at the supermarket, etc. Lists are useful for organization, studies, communication and memory, among other things.

THE AUTHOR

I love making lists. So I made a list of the things I would like to tell my dear readers:

1. This book had 82 different drafts. No kidding.

2. I had lots of fun writing this story.

3. It was also very, very, very hard work.

4. Many members of my family helped out.

5. I love Fuzz's and Charlotte's families.

6. I'm as quick as a hare when making up stories.

7. But I'm as slow as a tortoise when reading instruction manuals.

8. I've run out of items.

9. But I like lists that have nine items.

P.P.S.

Many different kinds of text were used in Fuzz's story, and we thought it would be interesting to talk about them in the P.S.

A text often has an objective. For example, the objective of a letter is to send a message; a biography tells the story of someone's life; and patient information leaflets tell consumers how to use a particular kind of medication. Depending on the objective of the text, the writing style varies. (We apologise for not mentioning this earlier, but birds and bunnies are scatterbrained creatures, who often forget what they're supposed to be doing.)

We would also like to thank the people who contributed ideas and suggestions, Claudia, Paulo, who wrote the song, Márcia Lígia Guidin, and Ângela Prado de Melo Aranha.

PUSHKIN CHILDREN'S BOOKS

We love stories just as much as you. Since we were very young, we have loved to hear about monsters and heroes, mischief and adventure, danger and rescue, from every time and every place.

We created Pushkin Children's Books to share these tales from different languages and cultures with you, to open the door to the colourful worlds beyond that these stories offer.

From picture books and adventure stories to fairy tales and classics, from fifty-year-old favourites to current huge successes abroad, Pushkin Children's books are the very best stories from around the world, brought together for our most discerning reader of all: you.

For more great stories, visit
www.pushkinchildrens.com